W9-AVK-637

Disney

MICKEY MOUSE CLUBHOUSE

Look and Find® WHAT'S DIFFERENT?

Written by Melanie Zanoza

Illustrated by Art Mawhinney

Additional illustrations by the Disney Storybook Artists

© 2009 Disney Enterprises, Inc. All Rights Reserved.

This publication may not be reproduced in whole or in part by any means whatsoever without written permission from the copyright owners. Permission is never granted for commercial purposes.

Published by
Louis Weber, C.E.O., Publications International, Ltd.
7373 North Cicero Avenue, Lincolnwood, Illinois 60712

Ground Floor, 59 Gloucester Place, London W1U 8JJ

Customer Service: 1-800-595-8484 or customer_service@pilbooks.com

www.pilbooks.com

p i kids is a registered trademark of Publications International, Ltd.

Look and Find is a registered trademark of Publications International, Ltd., in the United States and in Canada.

8 7 6 5 4 3 2 1

ISBN-13: 978-1-4127-1876-9
ISBN-10: 1-4127-1876-7

publications international, ltd.

Meeska, Mooska, Mickey Mouse!
Welcome to the Clubhouse. My pals and I are dancing along to the Hot Dog song! Can you spot us in our Anytime Area? Do you see what's different?

Pluto

Mickey

Minnie

Toodles

Daisy

Donald

We just flipped the Silly Switch to turn our Anytime Area into the kitchen to get ready for a picnic. Can you find the foods we're packing? Do you see what's different?

1 basket

2 apples

3 sandwiches   4 bananas   5 milk cartons   6 carrots   7 oranges

How will we get to our picnic? That's right—we'll take the Toon Car! Can you find some other ways of getting around? Do you see what's different?

Plane

Bicycle

Glove balloon

Hang glider

Wagon

Roller skates

Rocket

Oh, pickle juice! The Toon Car has a flat tire. Oh, Toodles! We're going to need a Mouseketool. How about this one? Do you see these other wrenches anywhere? Do you see what is different?

Heart-shaped wrench

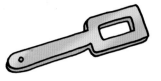

Rectangle-shaped wrench

   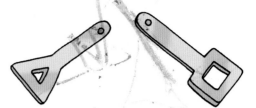

Circle-shaped wrench   Flower-shaped wrench   Diamond-shaped wrench   Triangle-shaped wrench   Square-shaped wrench

Can you help us find a great spot for our picnic? How about the Sandy Beach? No, it's too sandy! Before we keep looking, can you find these beach things here? Do you see what's different?

This umbrella

Sunglasses

Should we have our picnic in the Rain Forest? You're right — it's too wet here for a picnic. Do you see some creatures that love living here? Do you see what's different?

This anteater

This jaguar

This monkey
This snake
This butterfly
This frog
This toucan

The Toon Car has brought us to the frozen Arctic, but it's too cold here for our picnic. Can you spot some animals that are happy to live here? Do you see what is different?

This seal

This polar bear

 This penguin

 This caribou

 This puffin

 This walrus

Hot dog! We've arrived at Mickey Park...a perfect place for our picnic! Do you see these snacks in the park? Do you see what is different?

Box of raisins

Hot dog